THE STINKY TRUTH

To Mum, Dad, and Sis—
with memories of the Kingsdown Street Fair and loads of love

—J.B. x x x

MARGARET K. McELDERRY BOOKS
An imprint of Simon & Schuster Children's Publishing Division
1230 Avenue of the Americas, New York, New York 10020

MARGARET K. McELDERRY BOOKS is a trademark of Simon & Schuster, Inc.
For information about special discounts for bulk purchases,
please contact Simon & Schuster Special Sales at 1-866-506-1949
or business@simonandschuster.com.
The Simon & Schuster Speakers Bureau can bring authors
to your live event. For more information or to book an event,
contact the Simon & Schuster Speakers Bureau at 1-866-248-3049
or visit our website at www.simonspeakers.com.
Book design by Jack Noel | The text for this book was set in ITC Usherwood.
The illustrations for this book were rendered in pen and ink, and digitally.
Manufactured in the United States of America   1018 FFG
First Margaret K. McElderry Books edition November 2018
2   4   6   8   10   9   7   5   3   1

Library of Congress Cataloging-in-Publication Data
Names: Berger, Joe, 1970- author, illustrator.
Title: The stinky truth / Joe Berger.
Description: New York : Margaret K. McElderry Books, [2018] |
Series: Lyttle lies ; [2] | Summary: Sam Lyttle's mother will allow him to see
the first Wolfe Stone movie at the end of the summer only if he can avoid
telling a single lie until then.
Identifiers: LCCN 2018026945 (print) | LCCN 2018034761 (eBook)
ISBN 9781481470865 (hardback) | ISBN 9781481470889 (eBook)
Subjects: | CYAC: Honesty—Fiction. | Humorous stories. | BISAC: JUVENILE
FICTION / Comics & Graphic Novels / General. | JUVENILE FICTION /
Humorous Stories. | JUVENILE FICTION / Short Stories.
Classification: LCC PZ7.B4518 (eBook) | LCC PZ7.B4518 Sti 2018 (print) |
DDC [Fic]—dc23
LC record available at https://urldefense.proofpoint.com/v2/url?u =
https-3A__lccn.loc.gov_2018026945&d = DwIFAg&c = jGUuvAdBXp_
VqQ6t0yah2g&r = e7B1LsYfe_IOM7lAwBLqi7SXmy0k4CbOkBLKbHeKcD_
WwDNevNv1pxqPRmS0MUCm&m =
Bw-c51CuX9w2pBGH03b7f6DW3sPJ0XEmLlD0uzmWm4Q&s =
WTh63UDZgwxpTDdF6Fi2ZnA7unB0Kjq26mJoYXnsGIM&e =

LYTTLE LiES

THE STINKY TRUTH

JOE BERGER

MARGARET K. McELDERRY BOOKS

NEW YORK   LONDON   TORONTO   SYDNEY   NEW DELHI

Have you ever felt the weight of the world on your shoulders?

Have you ever wanted, desperately, to be able to turn back the clock, and do something differently—or not do something at all?

If you haven't, you're lucky.

It's the loveliest feeling to have nothing preying on your mind, no dark clouds looming. . . . I felt like that once—for just a few fleeting moments. Three weeks ago, at the beginning of the summer break . . .

It's been a stressful year, but my worries have evaporated with the coming of summer.

For a long time, the bane of my life was the school bully,

FEENY.

But since he got made to join the principal's Garden Gang, everything's changed. I have to hand it to the principal—it seems like his bizarre discipline technique actually has its merits, at least where Feeny's concerned. Feeny's gone from being a cheeseburger-munching school menace to a mild-mannered, salad-loving vegetarian.

FEENY THEN ➡ FEENY NOW

He's also had his hellhound Butcher rehomed, since he no longer believes dogs should be kept in the city. The only downside to all this is Feeny's show-and-tells, which are now looooong booooring lectures on sustainability (whatever that is) and vegan recipes.

So school is over for another year. And another, even MORE marvelous thing has happened. Drumroll, please . . .

We're **not** going on a summer vacation!!

Okay, so you're probably thinking that sounds like a bad thing, and I suppose it might be, under normal circumstances, but . . . double drumroll, please—Charlie's not going away either!!! Which means we get to spend the whole summer, every single hot, dusty, never-ending second of it, doing "that thing," what's it called? That important thing children need to do? Oh, yes, that's right—NOTHING! Hanging around to our hearts' content.

It gets even better. . . . In three weeks' time it's the neighborhood carnival.

NEIGHBORHOOD
CARNIVAL!
FLOATS!
MUSIC!
STALLS!
COSTUME PARADE!
OPEN-AIR CINEMA SCREENING!

Everyone is going to be involved, even my mom (though she doesn't know it yet (ahem)). It's going to be super-fun—and the absolute best thing about it is . . .TRIPLE drumroll—an open-air screening of *Cry Wolfe*. Charlie and I are officially the world's biggest fans of the greatest crime-fighter ever:

We follow the reruns on TV, but we've never had a chance to see the original made-for-TV, feature-length Wolfe Stone movie. It's super rare, and the chance to see it on the big screen is a once-in-a-lifetime opportunity.

Who knew we weren't the only Wolfe Stone fans in the neighborhood?

Technically, the summer break starts tomorrow. And the moment it starts; well, it's begun to end, hasn't it? That's why the last day of school is so special. It's limbo time, and I love every second of it. Of which there are approximately two hundred, before I walk through the front door, back to a reality splashdown. . . .

My dad spends 99% of his free time practicing his jazz-guitar noodling. Mom doesn't love jazz-guitar noodling roughly 110% of the time. So he's been banished to the plot. I think his feelings are a bit hurt, but he's putting a brave face on it. And Grandpa doesn't seem to share Mom's jazz allergy.

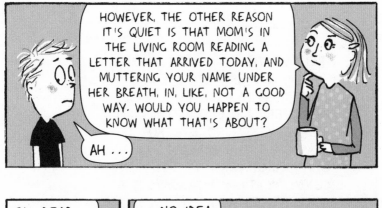

HOWEVER, THE OTHER REASON IT'S QUIET IS THAT MOM'S IN THE LIVING ROOM READING A LETTER THAT ARRIVED TODAY, AND MUTTERING YOUR NAME UNDER HER BREATH, IN, LIKE, NOT A GOOD WAY. WOULD YOU HAPPEN TO KNOW WHAT THAT'S ABOUT?

AH . . .

OH, DEAR . . .

. . . NO IDEA.

WHICH WOULD BE, I'M GUESSING, NOT ENTIRELY THE TRUTH.

PICTURE OF INNOCENCE

EXPLAIN, PLEASE.

LOOKS LIKE ... WORDS?

HERE, LET ME HELP. IT'S FROM THE CARNIVAL COMMITTEE.

SWIPE!

BLINK BLINK

Dear Mrs. Lyttle,

It is with great pleasure we contact you today.

You have been chosen to lead a "charity Zumbathon" in this year's Neighborhood Carnival. Your "Olympic-standard Zumba dancing" is bound to get everybody moving, and ensure the day is a huge success.

WOW! I HAD NO IDEA YOU WERE AN OLYMPIC ZUMBA DANCER.

I DON'T EVEN KNOW WHAT ZUMBA DANCING IS!

THAT MAKES TWO OF US.

THING IS, THEY CAME TO SCHOOL TO TALK TO US ABOUT THE CARNIVAL. DYLAN TOLD THEM HIS DAD CAN BLOW FIREBALLS WHILE PLAYING THE FLUTE.

DAISY SAID HER MUM WAS A TRAPEZE ARTIST. I JUST DIDN'T WANT YOU TO BE LEFT OUT.

SO YOU LIED!

WELL, NOT TECHNICALLY LYING, BECAUSE YOU ARE GOOD AT DANCING! AND YOU LOVE A CHALLENGE!

AND YOU LIED AGAIN, JUST NOW, WHEN I ASKED YOU ABOUT IT.

LET'S NOT GET OVEREXCITED HERE.

THIS IS ONE TINY THING, AND IT'S NOT EVEN REALLY A LIE — IT'S MORE OF A "TRUTH MAKE-OVER."

ONE TINY THING? YOUR RECENT PAST IS PRACTICALLY A FESTIVAL OF FIBS! WHAT ABOUT THAT TRAY OF SQUASHED DONUTS YOU "HAD NOTHING TO DO WITH"?

THAT WASN'T ACTUALLY ME! IT WAS MY BUM!

CAN I HELP IT IF MY BUM HEARS SOME MUSIC AND STARTS DANCING ME ALL AROUND THE KITCHEN?

UP ONTO A CHAIR AND THEN THE COUNTERTOP?

AND THEN LANDS ME SMACK-BANG IN THE MIDDLE OF A TRAY OF DONUTS?

Hear that? That's my "Suzy Sense."
It goes off when my big sis is onto me.
She (allegedly) only has my best interests at
heart—but she has a killer instinct for how
to hit me where it really, really hurts.

HE AND CHARLIE CAN'T WAIT FOR THIS "ONCE IN A (SAD PERSON'S) LIFETIME EXPERIENCE"— THEY'VE BEEN GOING ON ABOUT IT FOR MONTHS.

NO, NO!

AND NOW IT'S JUST THREE WEEKS AWAY.

NO, NO, NO! YOU CAN'T MAKE ME MISS THE SCREENING—THAT'S NOT FAIR! WE'RE NOT EVEN GETTING A PROPER SUMMER VACATION.

I KNOW I SAID THAT WAS A BONUS EARLIER—BUT IT'S GUILT-TRIP GOLD.

ALL RIGHT. THANK YOU, SUZY.

HERE'S THE DEAL, SAM.

Something is lurking there—something I've dumped in the deepest bargain bin of my mind . . . a faint shadow . . .

It never seems to occur to anyone that whistles can get grubby. . . .

That's my big sister, Suzy, always looking out for me.
Apparently.

Here's the thing. I don't lie out of some sort of principle. I'm not, like, a warrior monk of lying, wandering the world telling fibs.

IF YOU'RE GOING THAT WAY, MY FRIEND, BE CAREFUL. IT'S RAINING PUMPKINS.

Me, I'm more of a panic-liar. Accidents happen, and I don't want to get into trouble, so I have to "think on my feet."

Which is hard when your feet are busy running away as fast as they can.

But all that has to change. No more running away.

Now I must travel the

STINKY SWAMP OF TRUTH

Staying on the "straight and narrow" might sound easy enough—but in fact the path of truth is a treacherous health and safety nightmare.

Every way you turn, there are gloopy, eggy bogs,

and gassy sinkholes that could do you in.

They may be narrow, but the pathways through this nightmarish swamp are anything but straight.

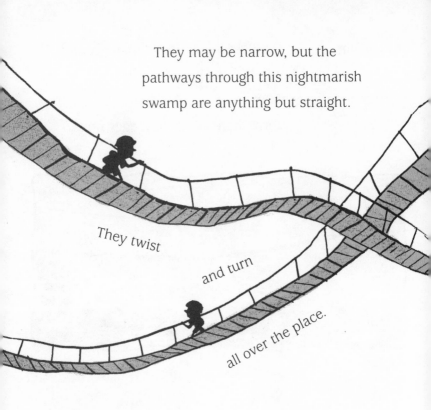

They twist

and turn

all over the place.

There are slats missing . . .

. . . and you never know when you might hit a dead end, and have to backtrack or improvise.

Am I prepared? Let's see . . .

I have no compass, or torch, or noseplugs.

I forgot to bring a waterproof jacket in case it rains.

At least I have lollipops. . . .

But I do know where I need to get to. Somewhere on the other side of this swamp, in three weeks' time, is a glorious fun-filled carnival, and an open-air movie-screening of the coolest crime-fighter the world has ever seen. And all I need to do is rise to the challenge before me, and stick to the truth.

TIME REMAINING TILL CARNIVAL

18 06 17

DAYS   HOURS   MINUTES

SAM, THE PUPIL VOTED "MOST LIKELY TO BECOME A HEADLINE ON THE EVENING NEWS."

OKAY, THAT IS TRUE — BUT I DON'T THINK IT WAS MEANT IN A GOOD WAY.

THESE PEOPLE, CHARLIE — THEY MISPRIZE MY GUMPTION.

THERE ARE AT LEAST TWO WORDS IN THAT SENTENCE I DON'T UNDERSTAND.

IN ANY CASE, IF YOU RUN INTO TROUBLE WITH THE CHALLENGE, YOU NEVER KNOW; MAYBE ALIENS WILL FINALLY ARRIVE ON EARTH AT SOME POINT DURING THE NEXT THREE WEEKS.

HOW WOULD THAT HELP?

Speaking of challenges. Dinner at home has become a bit challenging in itself, since Dad moved his jazz-guitar setup down to Grandpa's plot.

If you know my grandpa, you'll know how obsessed he is with radishes.

GRANDPA

RADISH

MASSIVE WEIRD ELECTROMAGNETIC ATTRACTION

Well, I'm afraid the obsession has worsened. As if raw radishes with cold butter and a pinch of salt weren't bad enough (Bleurgh!), now he also PICKLES the radishes!

PICKLED RADISHES!

PICKLED!?

RADISHES!?

One of the peculiar things about the neighborhood carnival is how many pickle stalls there are—you'd think "none" would be the ideal number, but instead we have two.

Muriel next door always runs a pickle stall, and so does Grandpa. But every year, Muriel's pickles sell out, while Grandpa has a lot of leftovers. He's determined to sell out this year; it's kind of a pride thing. I think Grandpa's secretly sweet on Muriel, and believes she could never love a man who can't sell his own pickles.

You should see his shed on the plot. It's lined with shelves and shelves of horrifying pickling experiments.

Imagine if, one night, a plucky ragtag band of radishes hauled themselves out of the ground and went looking for their comrades.

They'd creep under the door . . .

Flip on the light . . .

The scene that would greet them would be like something from a horror movie.

Thing is, Grandpa's also a self-taught magician, known as "**THE GREAT WONDEROSO**."

He taught himself how to disappear a parking ticket (no one's ever found it), and how to turn an orange purple (if you ever see a purple orange, don't eat it). And he taught himself the art of hypnosis—he claims to have successfully hypnotized the slugs on his plot to despise radishes. Maybe they're hypnotized, maybe they're just sensible? Anyway, the point is, he doesn't like to learn from books. He says:

He takes this same "no-instruction-manuals" approach with pickling—but you can't learn a lot from talking to a jar of pickled radishes. You have to use something called "trial and error." And that is, I'm afraid, what makes dinner so challenging. The "error" can be quite serious when all sorts of vile herbs, spices, and sweet and sour liquids are involved, and the "trial" part involves putting these things in your poor, unsuspecting mouth.

Oh, yes, there's something I forgot to mention. Grandpa's convinced that the secret to the elusive magical pickling formula is Dad's jazz-guitar noodling.

Since Dad moved his sound system down to the plot, the vegetables are growing bigger and faster and, apparently, tastier than ever before. Each batch of pickles is named after the tune that Dad was jamming whilst Grandpa tossed random stinky nasties into the pickling vat.

This is true—Dad's taste buds were zapped in a bizarre accident involving a faulty guitar amp and a lightning storm in the late 1990s. Which does make me question his usefulness as a pickling partner—no one else seems to be bothered, though.

So I'm off and running. . . .

Let's just hope this **STINKY SWAMP OF TRUTH** doesn't have too many creepy surprises in it.

If I'm honest . . .

. . . this "telling the truth" lark is actually pretty straightforward once you get into the swing of it.

WHAT DO YOU THINK OF THIS COLOR, SAM?

IT'S CALLED "WARM ELEPHANT."

HONESTLY? I THINK THEY SHOULD HAVE CALLED IT "COLORBLIND ELEPHANT."

TIME REMAINING TILL CARNIVAL

0 9 0 2 2 2

DAYS   HOURS   MINUTES

Telling the truth may be easy, but staying out of trouble can be harder—especially when you've got so much "nothing" to do.

I know, I know, I said I was really looking forward to doing nothing all summer—but that's only fun when it happens together with Charlie. And when he's not around because he's got to buy shoes or go to a silly wedding or whatever, time really starts to drag. And that's when accidents happen.

For instance, who could have foreseen that a simple piece of plastic tubing would create untold havoc?

Not me.

All I did was pick it up and whoosh it round my head a couple of times, and discover that it made a marvelous low, droning, whooshy sound.

LOW DRONING WHOOSHY WHOOSH...

(Well, actually, I did know this would happen. I have tried it once before.)

And how was I supposed to know that doing this in the living room would be a BIG mistake?

(Again, now that I think about it, that is what I did last time.)

But honestly—who would leave that stupid clock on the side table AGAIN where it could get knocked off onto the floor AGAIN and the glass face broken AGAIN?

Okay, the last time this happened I put the clock back on the table and ran away. When it was discovered, I denied any involvement. Which was "lying." So this time, when the exact same thing happens, I have a careful think.

I go to Mom, and explain what happened. Mom is very cross, and I will have to pay for the damage to the clock from my pocket money. But I have told the truth! I stayed on the right path.

TIME REMAINING TILL CARNIVAL

0 6   1 7   1 9

DAYS   HOURS   MINUTES

Meanwhile, everyone else is so busy that they keep out of my way.

Grandpa and Dad are rattling through many further iterations of pickle disaster,

Mom is rising to the Zumba challenge.

She's co-opted several of my friends' moms
(including Charlie's) to join the Zumba Moms charity
Zumbathon.

It is a little more ambitious than I had in mind when I mentioned it to the committee.

My friends are not thrilled about this.

Even Suzy's got the carnival bug. She's running a stall selling all her old toys—it's almost like she *wants* to grow up or something. Weirdo.

She's canvasing the neighborhood for old toys and games to sell at her charity stall—I imagine the spiel goes something like this:

Pudding, on the other hand, is not faring quite so well.

She has begun to produce the most heinous noxious gases, and her fur seems to be getting visibly lighter.

Mom takes her to the vet but she gets a clean bill of health.

I've even had to ban her from the den, which is where Charlie and I go to watch more excerpts from *Cry Wolfe*. . . .

CRY WOLFE

TIME REMAINING TILL CARNIVAL

0 3   1 6   0 6

DAYS   HOURS   MINUTES

The days are ticking by, but my troubled relationship with the truth continues to be put to the test. Even when Charlie is around, problems can still occur.

For instance . . .

Mr. EG (our name for him) is the old man who lives in the green house at the top of the road.

It's not an actual greenhouse—in fact it's not even green anymore, it's pale orange. But when it was green we called it "the green house"—"the pale orange house" doesn't sound right so we still call it the green house . . . we know what we mean.

We have long suspected him of being an Evil Genius (which is what "EG" stands for), so when we see him taking delivery of a sinister-shaped box . . .

. . . it's pretty obvious that it will contain components for a giant death ray.

SCREW AND ALLEN KEY FOR ATTACHING TO SATELLITE, ETC.

ACTUAL DEATH RAY BIT

REMOTE

All the signs are there:

SIGN 1:

The box says,

AUDIO/VISUAL PROJECTOR SCREEN

on the side, which is EXACTLY what you'd write on it if you didn't want people to know it was components for a giant death ray.

SIGN 2:

While we're going through his trash cans looking for evidence of evil plans, he jumps out at us and chases us away.

What's he trying to hide?

SIGN 3:

He somehow (spy satellite? network of informants (including my sister, perhaps)?) knows where I live, and comes to speak to my mom.

SIGN 4:

He is irrationally angry and upset about the mess we've made, another clear sign that he is up to no good.

My mom calls me and Charlie . . .

. . . we are hiding in a shoe chest at this point, listening in on the conversation to see if we have enough evidence to warn the government.

That's when Mom spots us. It's embarassing. It's awkward.

The old me would have tried to lie my way out.

I SWEAR — WE ONLY WENT IN HIS TRASH CAN BECAUSE WE SAW A LEPRECHAUN HIDING IN IT, AND I JUST WANTED TO RETURN THE POT OF GOLD TO ITS RIGHTFUL OWNER. . . .

The new me, the one who desperately wants to win the challenge, apologizes.

SORRY.

My mom is, again, fairly grumpy about the whole thing, but I did tell the truth. In any case, she's got more important things to do, like work out how to Zumba dance for three hours straight, in a week's time.

I'm pretty proud of her, actually—she's really going for it with the Zumba. She's so excited about it she's keeping a calendar where she marks off the days to the big event. At least I think that's what it's about.

So onward I plod through the bog, keeping my head down and my eyes on the prize.

And almost before you can say

it's the eve of the big day itself.

TIME REMAINING TILL CARNIVAL

022054

DAYS   HOURS   MINUTES

I've nearly done it. I've navigated a tricky path through the stinky swamp of truth; the mists are clearing, the bogs are drying out, and success is within sight.

Which is, of course, when it all goes horribly wrong.

SAM — A WORD, PLEASE.

OKAY.

FLOCCINAUCINIHILIPILIFICATION!

SIGH.

IT MEANS ...

YES ... THE ESTIMATION OF SOMETHING AS WORTHLESS, AND IT'S THE SECOND-LONGEST WORD IN THE ENGLISH LANGUAGE; YOU'VE DONE THIS ONE BEFORE.

So Charlie and I go to pick up the
package, little suspecting the disaster
that awaits. . . .

On the reverse of this mystery package is the return address—a vacation house we stayed at ages ago.

When I see it, a tiny alarm bell goes off in my head.

WE'RE ON A FAMILY SUMMER VACATION
IN A COTTAGE BY THE SEA.

SUZY'S BROUGHT HER BELOVED
CLOTHKITS DOLL, MOLLY.

ANYWAY, ON THE LAST DAY OF THE BREAK, I'M DRAWING AT THE TABLE, WITH MY FAVORITE PEN, GIVEN TO ME BY GRANDPA.

WHAT LOVELY DRAWINGS, SAM. BE CAREFUL WITH THAT MARKER PEN, THOUGH, IT'S PERMANENT, REMEMBER— DON'T GET ANY ON THE TABLE.

WHY YOUR GRANDPA THOUGHT THAT WAS A SUITABLE PEN FOR A CHILD IS A MYSTERY.

AND I SUDDENLY HAVE A BRILLIANT IDEA.

IT'S POSSIBLE I HAVE AN INFLATED
SENSE OF MY ARTISTIC ABILITY....

I'M NOT TOTALLY HAPPY WITH THE SMILE—
SO I HAVE ANOTHER GO AT THE MOUTH....

THEN THE EYES SEEM A BIT PENSIVE, SO I ADD
A BIT MORE LIFE TO THEM, AND THE CHEEKS....

AND THEN I THINK MAYBE THE FACE IS NOW A LITTLE OUT OF KEEPING WITH THE REST OF THE DOLL, SO I ADD A BIT OF DETAIL TO MAKE IT ALL FIT....

Sam Lyttle

All artistic commissions undertaken

No job too ambitious!

AND SUZY SAYS . . .

I WAS YOUNG — I DIDN'T UNDERSTAND THAT IT'S BEST TO GET THE ARTISTIC COMMISSION *BEFORE* YOU EMBARK ON THE WORK.

IN FAIRNESS, THE EXACT SAME THING HAPPENED TO MICHELANGELO WITH THE SISTINE CHAPEL CEILING. HE DID THE WHOLE THING AS A SURPRISE FOR POPE JULIUS II — HE HAD TO KEEP HIM FROM COMING INTO THE CHAPEL FOR FOUR YEARS* ...

YEAH, WELL, MICHELANGELO, Y'KNOW? PRETTY WELL REGARDED IN THE OLD PERMANENT MARKER DEPARTMENT. YOUNG SAM LYTTLE? NOT SO MUCH.

* this may not be true.

SO WHAT DID YOU DO?

WHAT ELSE COULD I DO? I MEAN, APART FROM CONFESSING.

Over time, Suzy forgot about Molly, and no one ever suspected I had anything to do with the disappearance—I gradually buried the awful thing I did in the deepest recesses of my mind. And now, like a ghost from the past, Molly has found her way home.

You know that bit in commercials on TV, when the person takes a bite of food they're not expecting to be nice and it actually is. They make a certain kind of face, like:

I'VE HEARD YOU PLAYING THE ZUMBA MUSIC AROUND THE HOUSE, AND THE RHYTHMS HAVE JUST NATURALLY INFUSED MY NOODLING.

WHAT ARE YOU DOING TOMORROW AT THE CARNIVAL, MARTIN?

WELL, I WAS GOING TO BE HELPING ON THE PICKLE STAND ... YOU KNOW, BIT OF INCIDENTAL JAZZ ...

YOUR WORK FOR ME IS DONE, MARTIN — I'M CONFIDENT THESE PICKLES WILL BE AN INSTANT SELLOUT.

163

I'VE GOT A LOT OF STUFF, AND THERE'S STILL MORE TO BE DROPPED AT THE STALL TOMORROW.

AREN'T YOU ... AREN'T YOU SAD TO BE SEEING THE LAST OF THESE TOYS?

NAH. NONE OF IT MEANS ANYTHING TO ME, NOT REALLY.

THERE WAS ONE DOLL I LOVED BUT ...

I LOST HER.

DON'T LOOK AT ME LIKE THAT.

WHAT IF ... THERE WAS A WAY TO GET MOLLY BACK?

IMPOSSIBLE. IT'S A GOOD LESSON, SAM. SOMETIMES YOU JUST HAVE TO LIVE WITH THE CONSEQUENCES OF YOUR ACTIONS. GROW UP, AND MOVE ON.

...CRACKLE...

...FSSST...

BTB TO WOLFE STONE—COME IN, STONE. OVER!

SUZY ... HOLD THAT THOUGHT!

You're probably thinking, "What's the big deal? You've won the challenge. You've even got a shiny new bike." But it's impossible to enjoy this stuff when there's something weighing on your conscience.

Just impossible.

CLICK!

DRAWN ON
STUBBLE

SCREEEECH!

GRANDPA THINKS THAT NOW THAT SHE HAS NO MORE PICKLE JUICE TO DRINK, SHE'LL GO BACK TO NORMAL.

BUT NOW THAT HE AND DAD HAVE WITNESSED THE AMAZING BLEACHING QUALITIES OF HER FARTS, THEY'RE GOING TO TRY TO RESURRECT THE RECIPE. THEY RECKON THE FORMULA FOR A MIRACLE STAIN-REMOVER GAS COULD BE WORTH A FORTUNE. IF THEY CAN STOP IT FROM STINKING....

Well, against the odds, I made it through the **STINKY SWAMP OF TRUTH**. I thought I was just looking forward to a movie, but it turns out I was after something a little bit more precious and hard to get hold of. A sense of contentment, the bliss of not being responsible for causing any bad stuff.

GUITAR DOWN, MARTIN.

POOF!

In my experience, moments like this never last long, but I'm going to savor every last second of it. . . .

Until the next inevitable homegrown calamity.